RAIN, RAIN, GO AWAY

Retold by STEVEN ANDERSON

Illustrated by MISA SABURI

CANTATA
LEARNING

WWW.CANTATALEARNING.COM

CANTATA LEARNING

Published by Cantata Learning
1710 Roe Crest Drive
North Mankato, MN 56003
www.cantatalearning.com

Library of Congress Control Number: 2015932815
Anderson, Steven
    Rain, Rain, Go Away / retold by Steven Anderson; Illustrated by Misa Saburi
    Series: Tangled Tunes
    Audience: Ages: 3–8; Grades: PreK–3
    Summary: In this twist on the classic song "Rain, Rain, Go Away," everyone
wants to go out and play. But the rain is making that hard to do.
    ISBN: 978-1-63290-360-0 (library binding/CD)
    ISBN: 978-1-63290-491-1 (paperback/CD)
    ISBN: 978-1-63290-521-5 (paperback)
    1. Stories in rhyme. 2. Weather—fiction.

Book design and art direction, Tim Palin Creative
Editorial direction, Flat Sole Studio
Music direction, Elizabeth Draper
Music arranged and produced by Musical Youth Productions

Printed in the United States of America in North Mankato, Minnesota.
122015   0326CGS16

ACCESS THE MUSIC!

SCAN CODE WITH MOBILE APP

CANTATALEARNING.COM

On rainy days you get stuck inside. You can't go out to play. And there are so many fun things to do outside. Sometimes, don't you wish you could tell the rain to go away and it would?

To try doing that, turn the page and sing along!

Rain, rain, go away.
Come again another day.

Daddy wants to play.
Rain, rain, go away.

Rain, rain, go away.
Come again another day.

Mother wants to play.
Rain, rain, go away.

Rain, rain, go away.
Come again another day.

Brother wants to play.
Rain, rain, go away.

Rain, rain, go away.
Come again another day.

Sister wants to play.
Rain, rain, go away.

Rain, rain, go away.
Come again another day.

My friend wants to play.
Rain, rain, go away.

Rain, rain, go away.
Come again another day.

Everybody wants to play.
Rain, rain, go away.

Rain, rain, go away.
Come again another day.

All my family wants to play.
Rain, rain, go away.

SONG LYRICS
Rain, Rain, Go Away

Rain, rain, go away.
Come again another day.

Daddy wants to play.
Rain, rain, go away.

Rain, rain, go away.
Come again another day.

Mother wants to play.
Rain, rain, go away.

Rain, rain, go away.
Come again another day.

Brother wants to play.
Rain, rain, go away.

Rain, rain, go away.
Come again another day.

Sister wants to play.
Rain, rain, go away.

Rain, rain, go away.
Come again another day.

My friend wants to play.
Rain, rain, go away.

Rain, rain, go away.
Come again another day.

Everybody wants to play.
Rain, rain, go away.

Rain, rain, go away.
Come again another day.

All my family wants to play.
Rain, rain, go away.

Rain, Rain, Go Away

World (Bossa Nova)
Musical Youth Productions

Verse 2
Rain, rain, go away.
Come again another day.
Mother wants to play.
Rain, rain, go away.

Verse 3
Rain, rain, go away.
Come again another day.
Brother wants to play.
Rain, rain, go away.

Verse 4
Rain, rain, go away.
Come again another day.
Sister wants to play.
Rain, rain, go away.

Verse 5
Rain, rain, go away.
Come again another day.
My friend wants to play.
Rain, rain, go away.

Verse 6
Rain, rain, go away.
Come again another day.
Everybody wants to play.
Rain, rain, go away.

Verse 7
Rain, rain, go away.
Come again another day.
All my family wants to play.
Rain, rain, go away.

GUIDED READING ACTIVITIES

1. The rain will not go away, and everyone wants to do something outside. Look at the beginning of this book. How is the little girl feeling? Do you ever feel like she does?

2. The dad is reading, but what would he like to be doing outside? The mom is working on her computer, but what would she like to be doing instead?

3. Draw a picture of what you would do on a rainy day.

TO LEARN MORE

Cannons, Helen Cox. *Rain*. North Mankato, MN: Heinemann-Raintree, 2015.

Cannons, Helen Cox. *Sunshine*. North Mankato, MN: Heinemann-Raintree, 2015.

Everitt, Melissa. *Rain, Rain, Go Away*. Oakville, ON: Flowerpot Press, 2013.

Manushkin, Fran. *Too Much Rain*. North Mankato, MN: Picture Window Books, 2010.